I0521450

Finding Bunny

A Grigsby Series Novella

Robert Maisano

Characters and events in this story are fictitious. Any similarity to real persons, living or dead, is coincidental and not intended by the author.

Biplane Media - San Francisco, California

www.robertmaisano.com

Copyright © 2017 by Robert Maisano

First Edition

ISBN-10:0-9994195-0-1
ISBN-13:978-0-9994195-0-2
10 9 8 7 6 5 4 3 2 1

Printed in the United States

For Animal Farm

Introduction

The idea behind the character of Grigsby Ives Pemberton and his subsequent adventures is an amalgam of experiences from growing up on Long Island's Gold Coast. The place where F. Scott Fitzgerald wrote The Great Gatsby, the part of New York where tycoons of industry celebrate their wealth, love of family, competition, and opulence.

When I was a kid, I'd read about Vanderbilt, Morgan, and Rockefeller. I envied their success but wondered if they ever laughed. Black and white photos of these Titans showed the same thing: stoic men with silly facial hair, holding the expression like a rod was stuck somewhere it shouldn't be. This confused me. Even at 5 years old I thought, "Do they ever have fun? They have everything they could want!" Perhaps the lack of antibiotics and air conditioning kept them crotchety.

This notion stayed with me as I grew. I've worked in the offices of the U.S. Capitol and for Fortune 500 Financial Institutions. When my other young colleagues spoke of the higher-ups with fear or wonder, I'd imagine them doing things completely differently. I'd ask my colleagues if they thought the boss would ever spend her money on having a miniature pig race, but the pigs all would have to wear top hats. The questions would be answered by a collection of misshapen faces.

I don't understand the people who cannot see the humor in the day-to-day. I guess we better leave them working on the bean counting and TPS reports. For the rest of us who would like to smile at points during the workweek, I've created Grigsby. A satirical series of an extremely wealthy man, with the appetite of a neurotic adolescent, who gets himself into strange situations. I've made the chapters very short, so they can fit into Instagram posts and on other platforms. The chapters can be read in quick hits, 1 to 3 minutes. Ideal for when you're hiding from your boss in the bathroom stall or waiting for that Uber that seems to be perpetually just a block away.

I'll work hard on providing the absolute best stories possible and ensure Grigsby never holds back.

Talk soon,

Robert Maisano
San Francisco, California

"If you can count your money, you don't have a billion dollars." - J. Paul Getty

"There are probably some things I could do to keep my flexibility up, but I'd rather smoke, drink diet Cokes and eat." - John Daly

CHAPTER ONE

Born on the Fourth of July

Meet Grigsby Ives Pemberton; his friends call him Grigs, his enemies call him other names. Grigsby's "pocket change" goes to caddies and strippers. Bad Days? He's never had one. Each morning begins with three espressos and a cigar the length of a zucchini. He chomps on it while reading the Wall Street Journal. He has a subscription to the New York Times but uses it only to line the parrot cage.

Grigsby has many cars but Muffy, his '68 Benz, is his top choice. It can be seen speeding along willow wack roads in Connecticut. Yes, Sinatra may be blaring from the car when he's with the family, but most of the time he bumps A Tribe Called Quest.

At a party once in Brooklyn, a woman with a brow ring and loud haircut asked what he identifies as. He shrugged and said a railroad tycoon born a century late. That doesn't mean he's a Luddite, quite the opposite. The Pemberton fortune is built on a variety of sources. Silicon resistors make up a large part along with holding the patent to the hamster wheel.

For the first time ever, we're going to take a look into Grigsby's life. He's been known to jaunt between Manhattan, New Canaan, and West Hampton all in one afternoon. His bulldog, Chunks, riding shotgun. Plus he's got unfinished business in San Francisco.

The following story, Finding Bunny, Grigsby will face obstacles he's never had to cross, and he won't always succeed. Let's go.

CHAPTER TWO

A Different Kind of Zen

There are two things Grigsby Ives Pemberton will wait for, tee-times and shoe shines. Anything else upsets him.

Grigsby parked his Bentley outside the yoga studio in TriBeCa. Ira, his attorney, and friend is inside seeking nirvana.

"Goddammit, where is he?" Grigsby said as he bit into a gooey croissant, flakes fell onto his suit, but he didn't care. He sipped coffee which had a splash or two of brandy in it. The boy who made the coffee had only almond milk to offer. Grigsby swiftly declined, and the barista asked him to stop laughing at his wool cap.

The doors opened to the studio. A platoon of skinny women with yoga mats slung over their backs marched out like soldiers. Behind them Ira followed, looking sweaty in his designer athletic clothes. He hurried to the car and did not look zen. Grigsby gave Ira a wink and unlocked the doors. Ira climbed in.

"You find Shiva in there?" Grigsby asked.

"What? No. Is your phone on? Have you seen the

3

news?" Ira asked.

Grigsby pointed at the navigation screen of the car which was somehow live streaming a golf match. "Spief got an eagle on the last three holes. He's an animal."

"No. It's your silk company, the one based in Manila. There's report of a hostile takeover by the workers."

Grigsby's eyes widened, and Ira couldn't tell if he was smiling or grimacing. "Sounds bad," Grigsby said as he started the car. The delicate hum of the engine muffled as the windows closed.

"We need to fix this, fast," Ira said.

"If we're going to talk business on a Thursday, I'm going to need at least two mimosas and crab cake eggs Benny." Grigsby hammered the accelerator down and launched down Chambers Street. The militia of yuppie girls leaped out of the way onto the ground to avoid the Bentley. Grigsby saw middle fingers in his rearview and chuckled. New Yorkers have a different kind of zen.

Grigsby turned onto the West Side Highway heading North. If he was going to talk business and have brunch, it sure as hell would be a place with linen napkins and frightened waiters. He smiled, "We're going to Jean-Georges. Get the plant manager on the phone. I have an idea that might work."

CHAPTER THREE

Gorillas & Mimosas

Grigsby and Ira sat across from each other at the Jean-Georges in Manhattan. Grigsby was sweating, but it was a good sweat. In front of him sat an oblong plate of Eggs Benedict, crab cakes and asparagus. An ambitious meal for 7 am.

"Miss," Grigsby said, waving at the waitress who tried to scurry by their table. "Something terrible has happened."

Ira shot an anxious look at Grigsby. He worried Grigsby was going tell her about their silk company. The staff was currently being held, hostage.

"What seems to be the problem Mr. Pemberton?" the waitress said.

Grigsby raised his empty champagne flute, turned it upside and frowned, "We're in need of more bubbly, it's an emergency."

The waitress gave a tired smile and took the empty champagne flute to be refilled.

"Grigs, what are we going to do about this Manila

situation? The whole factory is under siege. The workers have taken control, and all the primary staffs are hostages." Ira said.

Grigsby bit into a perfect bite of Canadian bacon and Morel Hollandaise. "I have a plan. Get me the number for the Manila Zoo, the one off Mabini Street, ask for Diwata."

Ira stared at his friend. "Grigs...what are you planning?"

"Do you want it fixed or not? I'm not telling those guys down on Wall Street with shiny foreheads that they can't get their favorite pocket squares anymore." Grigsby said some egg remained on his face.

"Here's your drink Mr. Pemberton," the waitress said as she placed a fresh mimosa on the table. "Is there anything else I can—"

"Chocolate cake please." Grigsby interrupted. "We need our energy for today." She nodded and headed back to the kitchen.

Ira slid the phone across the table, "It's ringing."

Grigsby downed the mimosa, belched, picked up the phone and headed toward the entrance. He could see the people walking by Columbus Circle as he spoke to the zoo manager. Ira could see Grigsby pacing, eccentrically waving his arms about. After about 15 minutes Grigsby hangs up and returns to the table.

"Ira we're going to have to wire some money to the Manila Zoo," Grigsby said while sliding back into his seat.

The chocolate cake was now set in front of Grigsby. He slid the phone to Ira and began chuckling as he dug his fork in for a bite.

"What deal did you make Grigs?" Ira asked.

Grigsby's laughter grew more boisterous. Other diners in neckties and pinstripes looked over at the commotion.

"What does man fear Ira?"

"That's a tall list. Taxes, in-laws, flu, divorce..."

"No, no, no, I'm talking about shit-your-pants-fear," Grigsby said biting into a warm piece of chocolate cake. Melting fudge dripped off the fork onto the white tablecloth.

Ira shrugged and said nothing.

"Beast," Grigsby said.

"Oh no Grigs, you didn't."

"As soon as you wire the funds" Grigsby looked at his Panerai watch, "Eleven gorillas will be released into the factory. That should get those protesters to back off."

CHAPTER FOUR

Disco Inferno

Grigsby unrolled his shirt sleeve and began placing stickers on his arm. One had a unicorn, the other a Dia de Los Muertos image and the last was a rainbow. Grigsby rested his head back in the Bentley seats and exhaled. Ira was driving.

"What are those stickers Grigs?" Ira asked.

"They heal me," Grigsby answered with his eyes closed.

Ira opened his mouth to speak but decided to let this one go. They had a successful brunch meeting. Releasing gorillas into the silk factory ended the hostage crisis. It's a good day when the Pemberton fortune is protected.

They were driving up Central Park West when Ira smelled smoke. He looked over at Grigsby who'd been asleep for some time now. Small embers seemed to be growing on his arm. Ira figured it was the sunlight reflecting off of his $18,000 watch. To be sure, Ira pulled over and checked his friend's arm.

Grigsby stirred awake screaming. His entire arm set ablaze.

"The center console, the center console dammit," Grigsby shouted.

Flustered, Ira opened up the center console, and condensation steamed out. It was a mini-freezer containing a bottle of Dom.

"Open it you monkey!" Grigsby said, swatting at the flame with his hand.

Ira tore the foil off and removed the wire cap but struggled to open the cork. Grigsby grabbed the bottle and bit into the cork. It popped open immediately; he spat the cork against the dash. Grigsby covered the top of the bottle with his thumb and began shaking it. A moment later it sprayed all over his arm, dousing the flames.

The fire was out. Ira opened the windows to let out all the smoke. It smelled exactly like a Miami night club, stale champagne, and burnt hair.

"My tailor is going to weep when he sees this; you know this suit is bespoke?" Grigsby said. He took his jacket off and tossed it in the backseat.

"We need to get you to the hospital Grigs," Ira said.

"No way, it's amateur hour over there. Where are we?" Grigsby stuck his head out the window, looking for a street sign. "Go two blocks north. My barber, Luigi can patch me up. He's used to helping his New Jersey friends with much more severe wounds if you know what I mean."

"Oh man I hate Luigi," Ira said, wringing the leather steering wheel.

"Drive Ira," Grigsby said, "Plus he might have gelato."

"He better," Ira said, he put the car in drive and drove north.

"Also get Gwyneth on the line, I have to talk to her about these stickers."

CHAPTER FIVE

The Barber of 72nd Street

Ira double parked the Bentley outside Luigi's Barbershop. Grigsby hopped out. He entered the barber shop which was small and only fit three plush chairs. It smelled of Pinaud-Clubman aftershave and talcum powder. Pavarotti played softly from old speakers.

Ira wasn't sure if Grigsby was speaking Italian or reciting lines from a Fellini film. Either way, Luigi smiled when he saw Grigsby. Luigi looked like every elderly Italian man who immigrated to New York City. Full head of white hair, leather skin the color of bourbon and sinewy but healthy.

"Grigsby, mio dio, what happened?" Luigi asked. He set down an espresso and croissant to examine the burns on Grigsby's arms.

"I was trying to live my truth," Grigsby said, "Can you fix me up?"

"Of course, sit, please," Luigi said. He looked at Ira, "Ira make yourself useful and draw the shades and lock the front door."

Ira rolled his eyes, "Good to see you too Luigi."

Luigi took out an old medic kit from a cupboard and set it next to the scissors. Grigsby leaned back in the chair and exhaled. Luigi cut the remains of Grigsby's shirt sleeve.

"There goes $600," he said chuckling.

Luigi dabbed iodine along the burns and Grigsby yelled. Ira looked over with concern.

"Silencio," Luigi said. He grabbed his croissant and stuffed into Grigsby's mouth like a pacifier. Grigsby's grin stretched to both sides of the pastry.

Time passed, and soon the barber was bandaging Grigsby's arm. Ira went to the Bentley's trunk to retrieve a Rimowa briefcase. He returned and set the briefcase on an empty chair. Grigsby's initials were embossed in gold.

"What's the combo?" Ira asked.

Grigsby turned and stared at his friend with a sly glint.

Ira shook his head and dialed the numbers to read 666. The briefcase popped open. Inside were hermetically sealed Thomas Pink Oxford shirts. Along with brass collar stays, cufflinks of bananas, silk pocket squares and a Mont Blanc fountain pen.

Grigsby jumped from the chair and started dressing. Moments later he was back to being, "100% Grigsby Ives Pemberton," as he said to the mirror. Grigsby helped himself to hair gel and other lotions on the counter.

Luigi smiled, he was happy to help a man he's known for decades. The smile faded when the front door opened and two burly men stepped in. They wore sweaters with horizontal stripes and gold chains and reeked of pastrami. Ira turned to the men and looked away fast.

"Oh no. Grigs," Ira whispered, "The Russians are

here."

CHAPTER SIX

Opera, Pie and the Russians

Grigsby was happy that his fresh bandage hid well under his shirt sleeve. The happiness vanished when he realized the two Russian men were sent by a business rival. The Pemberton empire is under constant assault from rivals, but this man was on the top of Grigsby's shit list.

"Pemberton, you know why we're here," one of the Russian's said.

Grigsby said nothing. Instead, he drank Luigi's espresso and sighed.

"Pemberton," the Russian said again.

"What does The Bear want now?" Grigsby asked.

"Don't play dumb Pemberton; we know it's you who outbid us last week in the new business venture in Brighton Beach."

"Hey, Captain Drago, do you know how many deals I make in a day? Branson and Cuban wish they had my speed. So get specific, or I'll have Ira kick both your asses."

Ira shot a worried look at Grigsby, like a puppy

knowing he was going to the vet for a final visit. Grigsby pursed his lips and gave him a don't worry wave.

The Russians were snickering. Then one said, "The Piroshki company, the...how-do-you-say...mini-pies?"

"Mini-pies! Of course, I remember now, who doesn't love pie? One second." Grigsby took a small notebook with a purple triangle on the cover from his pocket and flipped through the pages with haste. "Ah yes, here it is, the Novosibirsk Piroshki Company. They were looking to sell for $1.2 million, I had an associate there to bid on my behalf, but we didn't end up doing it."

The Russian duo exchanged confused looks. Grigsby flipped through more pages.

"Gentlemen, you were given the wrong information. It was, in fact, Randolph Scout Bishop the...fourth or fifth, who can keep track with that family dynasty." Grigsby said.

The Russians said nothing.

"Tell The Bear to get his facts straight and not waste my time," Grigsby said, he sat down in the barber chair. "Luigi, can I have a hot shave please?" Grigsby asked.

"Of course," Luigi said. He prepped the razor, towels and turned on the machine that warms the shaving cream.

"And crank up Pavarotti. I want to sing with him." Grigsby took a warm towel from Luigi and lay it over his eyes. The Russians were still standing there confused. Moments later Grigsby was belting out Nessun Dorma. Luigi shaved carefully and tried not to cut him with the straight razor. Grigsby is the only customer that sings opera while getting shaved. A dangerous habit.

The Russians threw up their hands and left. Ira did his

best to give a scowl, but it wasn't noticed by anyone.

Grigsby finished strong and maintained a vibrato finale as if he were side by side with Pavarotti. Luigi shed a tear; it was truly remarkable. Grigsby heard the door shut and took the towel off his eyes.

"They're gone," said Ira. "What the hell was that all about? Why'd your throw Randolph under the bus?"

"He was a prick lacrosse player in boarding school. I love throwing chance obstacles in his way." Grigsby said chuckling. "Anyway, we need to go."

"Why?" Ira asked.

"Because I, in fact, did buy the mini-pies company. I mean who says no to pie? Lunatics that's who. Anyway, once The Bear figures out we duped his men, he's going to be upset."

"Should we head to the Manor?"

"We'll get there soon, but first we need to do a preemptive strike. Luigi, where's the nearest pet store?" Grigsby asked.

Luigi shrugged.

"Fine, where's the nearest pizza joint?"

Luigi smiled, "One block down."

"Excellent," Grigsby stood, tossed a wad of cash on the counter, hugged Luigi and kissed his cheek. "Ira, we're going to need a shoebox, a large pepperoni pizza, and sleeping pills. Let's move!"

CHAPTER SEVEN

Hats for Rats

The pizza place Luigi recommended looked like a dilapidated bank from the 1970s. It was narrow with sticky pseudo-brick floors. The ovens had a brownish-green patina along them from years of continuous use. Despite the shabby interior, it smelled glorious.

Grigsby looked like a toddler who just discovered melted cheese. He was in the process of rolling 2 slices of pizzas together to make a "pizza-urrrito" as he called it. Ira shook his head and continued to eat his slice with a knife and fork. They were waiting for their pepperoni pie to go.

"Pizza rat?" Ira asked. Grigsby nodded with a full mouth, chewing slowly like a cow.

"Everyone loves pizza, even rats," Grigsby said and belched, "So, we're going to go catch some. You have the sleeping pills?"

Ira nodded and bit into a small slice of cheese.

"Great, grind them up," Grigsby said, handing him a spoon.

"Gotta fresh pie on da counta ova'er." shouted a sweaty Italian man who looked like he'd been living off of calzones his whole life.

Grigsby scarfed down the rest of his pizza-urrito and grabbed the hot cardboard pizza box. He went outside to the Bentley which was parked in a fire lane. A meter maid was standing in front of it. After a minute of discussion, Grigsby had her laughing, two minutes later she was taking a slice of pizza from the box and tearing up the ticket.

They drove to Central Park. Grigsby refused to go into the subways claiming he's never been in one before. "Plus the Park has elegance," he said.

Grigsby took a seat by an old black man playing Miles Davis' Flamenco Sketches on a tarnished trumpet. Ira went off to set the trap.

An hour passed and the old man played through Davis' hits. Grigsby left $100 in the man's case. Ira reluctantly went to check back on the trap; he was muttering something about being top of his class at Yale Law School. Grigsby waited in the Bentley. Ira came by holding the box and set it in the trunk. He squirted an entire bottle of hand sanitizer in his palms afterward.

"How'd we do?" Grigsby asked. His navigation screen was streaming a live golf game in Pebble Beach.

"7 rats," Ira said.

"Good haul, I wonder if there's a business for supplying rats to people..." Grigsby said. He watched Mickelson miss a three-foot putt. "Anyway, we're on the move; we need to get going before our 7 new friends wake up."

"Where are we going Grigs?" Ira groaned.

"The Russian Tea Room."

"Oh Grigs, what the hell? No. We're not going. We can't go."

"I need my chicken kiev and Belvedere," Grigsby said.

"The Bear owns that place now; he's the head chef!"

"Exactly, chef, so he'll be in the back. No one will see us."

Ira continued to argue while Grigsby drove downtown. He pulled over at a Louis Vuitton on Madison Avenue and ran inside. Moments later he came outside tearing the tags off of a brown leather duffle bag.

"Put the rats in here," Grigsby said, tossing the bag in the car. He ran across the street to a pet shop and came out with miniature Russian fur hats. "Thank God for insane cat people, they had every small hat imaginable in there, stove top hats, sombreros, yamakas..." He gave Ira seven miniature hats and told him to affix it to their heads. Ira gave up on arguing and did what he said.

Ira was chuckling by the time he put the last hat on the final rat. "You're insane Grigs," Ira said.

Grigsby lit a cigar, "Incorrect. When you're as wealthy as I am you're eccentric, not insane. Look at Carrot Top, that guy is insane."

The Bentley's shadow grew long as the afternoon turned golden. Grigsby and Ira drove to The Russian Tea Room with their bag of rats wearing small hats. What they didn't know was their little prank would cost them dearly.

CHAPTER EIGHT

Escape the Russian Tearoom

The shattering of glass is what the diners heard first. Then they saw a plump man in a herringbone blazer sprinting out of the Russian Tea Room in Manhattan. The chef chased him, holding a "damn meat cleaver" as Grigsby put it.

The valet saw Grigsby sprinting out and tossed him the keys to the Bentley. Ira was halfway in the car when it peeled out of there leaving smoke in its wake. The chef chased them down 7th avenue. Grigsby and Ira thought fireworks were sounding nearby but realized it was the popping of a pistol.

"The Bear owns a gun?" Ira asked as he yanked on the seatbelt.

"Sounds like it. Don't worry. The car's retrofitted with bulletproof glass." Grigsby said, "Those James Bond marathons I watched as a kid served me well."

They drove north out of the city. Grigsby pressed a mahogany button, and a small humidor emerged from above the glove box. "Cuban?"

"No, goddammit Grigs that was close," Ira said.

"Suit yourself," Grigsby said. "Pass the torch will you?"

Ira complied and handed him the pistol-grip butane lighter. A sharp blue flame cooked the end of the cigar. Grigsby took a drag and opened all the windows. He looked at his nervous friend.

"Counselor..." Grigsby's eyebrows raised.

"Oh don't counselor me Grigs," Ira said.

Grigsby pouted, "Fine," They drove in silence for a long time until Ira spoke.

"How did you even meet The Bear?" Ira asked.

"I pissed him off a few years ago when I took something from him…" Grigsby answered. "Besides nukes, warmth, and blondes what are the Russians always seeking?"

Ira shrugged.

"Vodka," Grigsby answered.

"Oh Jesus, you didn't—"

Grigsby's grin stretched from ear to ear. "That's right."

Ira put his palms against his eyes. "No, no, no, no,"

Grigsby started laughing. "Bit of a hostile takeover. The Bear was the owner of a vodka company I acquired."

"And now you've decided to do this again to him with the pie company."

Grigsby nodded, exhaling smoke against the suede dashboard. "I guess I didn't really bury the hatchet tonight?" He said chuckling.

Earlier that evening, Grigsby and Ira brought the duffle bag of sedated rats wearing tiny hats into the Russian Tea Room. When the rats woke up, they all scurried for the kitchen. Most diners didn't notice. But the Bear, who's also the head chef, saw the tiny fur hats on the rats and knew of one man who would do this. Grigsby.

"Are we heading to the manor?" Ira asked.

"Not yet. I don't know about you, but the past hour has given me heartburn. We need to relax, decompress, and meditate maybe. And then head to Connecticut."

Ira sighed, "Where then?"

Grigsby gave him a look Ira knew too well. A half hour later Grigsby was surrounded by three strippers in lucite platform heels. Glitter covered Grigsby's face, and one of the strippers wore his herringbone jacket. Ira threw an ice cube at Grigsby to get his attention.

"Ira! Have you met Coco? She's from Paris." Grigsby asked.

"I didn't know Staten Island renamed itself."

"What?"

"Nothing, Grigs, we need to sort out what we're going to do with this vodka company and the pie company. If the Bear is that upset, things are only going to get worse." Ira said as he shooed away another dancer. He hated places that smelled like brass polish and hairspray.

Grigsby took out a stack of cash and made horizontal chops against it making it fly in the air. "Look I'm a sprinkler!" All the ladies cheered.

Ira stood up and went to grab Grigsby but sank in his seat when he saw The Bear walking by the bar.

"Grigs he's here," Ira said.

Grigsby turned and spotted him. The Bear was ordering a drink. "Okay, okay. Girls come here." They leaned in, and Grigsby whispered in their ears and gave them more cash. A moment later they were surrounding The Bear as Grigsby and Ira slipped out the rear exit.

Back in the Bentley, Ira made a few calls to his

paralegals. Grigsby wiped the glitter off his face with a monogrammed handkerchief.

"Okay, good, see you soon." Ira hung up the phone. "One of my people, who speaks Russian, can be at the manor by 2 am," Ira said sitting back into the plush leather seats and exhaling a sigh of relief.

"See Ira; it'll be fine." Grigsby tossed the handkerchief in the backseat and swore he saw something grab it. He tossed the car in gear and drove north toward the Hutchinson River Parkway.

Twenty minutes later Ira asked, "You smell that?"

Grigsby made a foul face. "Yes. What the hell..."

They both turned and looked in the backseat at a leather gym bag that hadn't been there before they entered the strip club.

"Whose bag is that?" Ira asked. He leaned back to grab the handle and noticed it was moving. A small furry hand, with thumbs, reached out and slowly began unzipping the bag. "What the fu—"

Grigsby's eyes widened as he watched a spider monkey in the rearview mirror leap from the bag screaming.

CHAPTER NINE

Somewhere in Greenwich

Grigsby swerved off the road as the monkey hollered from the back seat of the Bentley. The car skidded to a halt, and Ira jumped out and rolled to the ground. Grigsby followed shouting "Abandon ship!" He had a look of terror on his face but was laughing.

The Bentley's ice blue headlights cut through the night. They were within Greenwich, Connecticut's town limits near a golf course. Then again, you're always near a golf course in Greenwich. Besides the idling motor and wailing cries of a South American Spider Monkey, the night seemed peaceful. Ira and Grigsby stared at the car.

"Did The Bear do this?" Ira asked.

"Of course," Grigsby said, he tapped the window, and the monkey bore its fangs. "An eye for an eye." He chuckled.

Ira looked down the damp road, "Where the hell are we?" he said, squinting into the night.

"Get Ryuki on the line," Grigsby said. "Tell him we need a lift from the Round Hill Golf Club."

Ira shook his head, "Where's that?"

Grigsby pointed to a low-lying green, "That's hole 5, we're about 200 yards west from the clubhouse. C'mon let's go, the bar may still be open."

"What about the Bentley? It could get stolen."

"Ira, we're in Greenwich, the only crime that goes on here is white-collar. Plus, who's going to touch the car with a crazed monkey in it?" Grigsby said, "Plus it's insured."

The duo walked along the damp golf course. A crow cawed somewhere in the darkness. Ira told Ryuki, Grigsby's Butler, of the situation and said he'd be there soon. Grigsby interrupted the call and requested the chariot.

The clubhouse was locked when they arrived. Ira sat on a bench and closed his eyes. Grigsby remained against the door, and a moment later it popped open. Ira gave him a confused look.

"What? Don't you know how to pick a lock? I'll be back in a second." Grigsby said, disappearing into the dark building. A few minutes later he returned with two crystal tumblers. "The oldest they have is 12 year Balvenie. Savages." They clicked glasses and sipped in silence.

A half hour passed until they heard the low rumbling of what sounded like an airplane engine. Two yellow headlamps appeared at the end of the long drive. A metallic beast ambled toward them. Ryuki was behind the wheel.

"There she is," Grigsby said with pride. A vintage Duesenberg sedan pulled up, and Ryuki hopped out and opened the rear doors, his face stoic. Ryuki is a descendant of samurai lineage and maintains certain disciplines. This is why Grigsby has kept him as his confidant for two decades.

Grigsby left a $100 bill in the empty tumblers and set them on the bench. Moments later they were barreling through the wooded roads of Connecticut.

Ira hung up his phone, "My people are waiting at the Manor."

Grigsby nodded, "Great, we'll be there soon, we're going to need all the help we can get."

CHAPTER TEN
Trouble

The Duesenberg cut through forest roads en route to Pemberton Manor. Grigsby and Ira were in the backseat, Ryuki drove. Even though the car was over a half century old, the interior was quiet. Grigsby had it retrofitted with sound insulation used in recording studios. The occasional noise was from a champagne crate that sat near Grigsby.

"Shall we open some bubbly?" Grigsby asked.

Ira, who looked paler than normal said, "No. It's 2 am, and I feel like I'm going to vomit."

"Pity," Grigsby said, examining the bottle, "These are Boërl & Kroff Brut, they're delicious."

"How much longer Ryuki?" Ira asked.

Ryuki looked in the mirror, "Not long," he said, squinting from the high-beams of a car behind them.

"Okay, I'm going to try and get some rest," Ira announced.

"Sleep tight my sweet prince," Grigsby said, brushing Ira's cheek with the back of his hand. Ira swatted him

27

away.

The car behind them was tailgating now. Ryuki was getting annoyed, mumbling "go around," but the car remained fixed to their bumper.

Grigsby looked out the rear window, "What's the deal with this guy—"

The passenger leaned out the window and was holding a ball of flame. The flaming object was thrown at the Duesenberg. It shattered against the trunk, blanketing the rear in the fire. Grigsby and Ira yelled.

"The Russians!" Grigsby shouted. "They're tossing Molotov cocktails."

"Hang on," Ryuki said with calm, He punched the accelerator, and the howling of the V12 engine masked Ira's screams. The fire soon died out, but the headlights followed.

"Ira, hold on to me," Grigsby said, leaning out the window. He was holding a bottle of champagne and in a clean underhand throw tossed it in the air. The bottle sailed through the night and connected with the windshield. The car swerved but stayed on the road.

"Good shot Grigs," Ira said.

"I need another bottle," Grigsby said.

Ira armed him with one, then Grigsby shouted at Ryuki in perfect Japanese. Ryuki nodded. Grigsby underhanded the bottle again and it broke through the windshield.

Ryuki immediately killed all the lights to the Duesenberg and went invisible in the darkness. Ira and Grigsby felt the car turn sharply off the road onto a gravel path. They didn't know how Ryuki was able to see this well in the pitch of the night. Grigsby watched the

Russians continue down the main road. He smiled and looked at Ira.

"Well done Grigs," Ira said.

"And people say playing corn-hole is a stupid game."

CHAPTER ELEVEN

Pemberton Manor

Ryuki drove out of the fields and back onto a two-lane road. He turned on the yellow headlights and continued for Pemberton Manor. They had escaped the Russians by driving through back roads and farmland without headlights. Grigsby and Ira couldn't believe how Ryuki was able to see in total darkness.

"We're ten minutes away sir," Ryuki said.

Grigsby nodded, he was eating Tates chocolate chip cookies, two at a time. He wouldn't share any with Ira.

Tall wrought iron gates opened as the Duesenberg approached. Pemberton Manor was built during the time railroads were sprawling across America. Ellison Kingsley Spruce Pemberton, Grigsby's great-great grandfather, battled Rockefeller for the land. Ellison won. He commissioned the greatest architects of the time to build the family estate.

The Manor has Châteauesque elements and brilliant stonework. The grounds make greens keepers weep from the labor and beauty. Grigsby modified only a few areas of the Manor between the time of reading Batman comics and receiving access to his trust fund. There's rumor of a cave somewhere on the grounds. But only Grigsby, Ryuki and a few women who've signed NDAs have seen the modified areas.

Grigsby and Ira hopped out of the Duesenberg and went inside while Ryuki brought the car to the motor-pool. Moments later they were in the oak paneled study. The room was dimly lit and smelled of cinnamon and cigars.

Two nervous paralegals had been waiting there for over an hour. Grigsby was suspicious when they both declined a glass of Pappy Van Winkle. He told Ryuki to whip up some chocolate soufflés and a Baked Alaska. Ryuki nodded and disappeared into the kitchen.

"What are your names?" Grigsby asked.

The redheaded spoke first, "I'm Peter," he said, making it sound like a question.

"And I'm Caitlyn." she said, sounding more confident than Peter.

Grigsby shook both of their hands, being sure to crush Peter's a bit more. They sat and got down to business. Grigsby lit a fire in the wood-burning stove beside his desk. The hearth warmed the room, and the piney aroma made Grigsby think of Christmas. He hoped he'd see his family soon.

An hour passed and the grandfather clock tolled at 4 am. Grigsby ate two chocolate soufflés and forced Peter to eat the Baked Alaska. He said introverts should eat more than necessary and wear brighter colors. Peter's gums were stinging from the amount of sugar and cream he consumed. His face was beginning to match his hair.

Ira kept the meeting moving. They decided on a direction to take with the two companies Grigsby stole from the Russians. It would be tricky, but it seemed like the most profitable direction.

The rotary phone atop Grigsby desk rang. It was Ryuki calling from the security room.

"Yes?"

"Mr. Pemberton our proximity alarm picked someone up at the gates,"

"And?"

"Sir, it seems," Ryuki cleared his throat, "The Bear is at the gate."

CHAPTER TWELVE

Wake Up Crockett

"Let The Bear into the manor," Grigsby said.

"Are you sure sir?" Ryuki asked.

"Do it."

"Very well,"

"Wait, are you armed?"

"Always sir,"

"Good and wake up Crockett, dress him something frightening." Grigsby hung up.

Ira and his two paralegals, Peter and Caitlyn, stared at Grigsby as if he sealed their fates.

"Don't worry. We have home field advantage, Ryuki will frisk them at the door." Grigsby sat and licked the empty bowl that once held a chocolate soufflé.

"Who is Crockett sir?" Caitlyn asked.

"The greens keeper, he lives in the cottage beyond the barn. Big as an ape, he might be a part ape," Grigsby said.

Ira looked at Caitlyn, "Grigsby hired him because of his name."

Caitlyn gave a quizzical look.

"Miami Vice, jeez kids today don't have taste," Grigsby said.

They went to the Stagg Room. Pemberton Manor has several dining rooms. This one is adorned with busts of Elks, Gazelles and other animals. Grigsby took a seat at the head of the table, underneath a giant Grizzly bear. Ira smirked.

The Bear walked in with the two Russian men Ira and Grigsby met earlier today. Ryuki and Crockett were standing beside them. Crockett did not look happy. Grigsby put his hand on his face when he saw what Ryuki dressed him in.

Crockett, who was the size of a vending machine, somehow fit into a samurai suit of armor. He wore a half-face mask that covered him from nose to chin. The mask was brass and had ornate beast features.

"Pemberton." The Bear said, standing in front of the long mahogany table.

No one spoke. Flames flickered atop silver candelabras.

Grigsby stood up and spoke just above a whisper, "Here's how it's going to be. If we're going to have a civilized discussion, you need to follow house rules." Grigsby paused. "And if you cannot do that, Crockett will eat you."

Crockett turned and starred at The Bear. His guards tried staring down Crockett but quickly looked away.

"Okay." The Bear said, taking a seat at the table.

"Good. We have a proposition for you. Peter hands The Bear the documents."

Peter, the paralegal, didn't look well, he was recovering from being force fed the Baked Alaska. He slid the documents across the table.

"Now, I assume your Soviet ass can hardly read the Queen's English, so let me summarize what this says. The vodka company will remain under Pemberton Investments management. We'll provide 0.02% of the profits to you if you agree to have it stocked in your restaurants in Manhattan."

"0.02%? Is this a joke?" The Bear said.

"I don't think you're grasping exactly how much vodka is drunk by Connecticutians. It's their warm up drink."

The Bear shrugged.

"Pemberton Investments will start making the vodka in Connecticut and not near that gulag it's currently being made in. We're going to rebrand away from that Stalinesque name and give it something trendy. I'm thinking *Spruce Cove*. This will make the lacrosse moms buy it by the crate. We'll add the locally made, conflict-free, gluten-free, kale free, all that crap on the label. It'll essentially be rubbing alcohol in a pretty bottle sold at a 400% markup."

"Okay. Fine. Now the Piroshki company you stole—"

Grigsby tossed a folder across the table. It bore the company seal. The Bear opened it and his eyebrows raised.

"What the hell is this a photo of?" The Bear asked.

"A goose egg."

The Bear was growing red, a blue vein sprouted in the center of his brow and flowed to his hairline.

"You get nothing because no one touches my pies," Grigsby said.

The Bear stood slamming his fists against the table. He was shouting in Russian; spit flew across the room.

Grigsby was chuckling. The Bear looked for his two men and noticed they had vanished along with Ryuki.

"Behave you lunatic," Grigsby said. But The Bear kept shouting. "Crockett."

The Bear turned to see the Goliath in samurai armor approaching slowly. An instant later The Bear was unconscious.

CHAPTER THIRTEEN

Hot Air

Crockett, the massive greens keeper who was clad in samurai armor, stood over the unconscious Russian. Ira and his paralegals were in awe from the speed at which Crockett subdued The Bear.

Ryuki returned to the room with a single bead of sweat on his temple. He managed to take out the two Russian men who were guarding The Bear, yet no one saw how.

Grigsby stood with his hands on his hips nodding approvingly. "Well, they won't be receiving the invite to my Christmas party."

Ryuki looked at Crockett, smirked and then looked at Grigsby, "Sir, what would you like to do with them?"

"Are you going to kill them?" Peter the paralegal asked.

The room fell silent. Everyone looked at Peter.

Grigsby spoke, "Jeez Peter, we're not Italians. We're going to deal with this how all WASPs deal with their problems, stuff them away in the corner of the attic and never speak of them again."

Peter nodded and stayed quiet.

"Ryuki, do we still have the hot air balloon from the Fourth of July party?" Grigsby asked.

"Yes sir. It's in the barn."

"Good. You and Crockett bring it out to the field and get that thing ready."

"Why do you have a hot air balloon?" Peter asked.

Grigsby was now annoyed, "Read the Count of Monte Cristo and come back to me and ask me why not."

A red sun peaked on the horizon and dyed the whole sky cantaloupe. The air felt cold, but the sun was warm. Grigsby sent Ira and his two paralegals to the guest wing to get some sleep. Ryuki and Crockett readied the hot air balloon and then placed The Bear and his two men inside. They tossed in blankets, bottles of water and a box of mini meat pies from the company Grigsby stole from The Bear. They also gave them earplugs.

Ryuki fired up the igniter for the hot air balloon. Twenty minutes later a glorious yellow and red balloon inflated beside Pemberton Manor. Grigsby couldn't stop laughing. Even Crockett sneaked a grin.

The basket began to lift off of the ground. "Oh, one last thing," Grigsby said, reaching into his Barbour coat. He pulled out a small outdoor speaker connected to an iPod.

The balloon sailed away over the Connecticut sunrise. The speaker blared one German song from 1984 on a continuous loop that sang about of 99 red balloons.

CHAPTER FOURTEEN

Guests of Guests May Not Bring Guests

Grigsby stirred awake from the afternoon sunlight peeking through his Venetian blinds. He rolled (literally) out of his double Californian King mattress and descended the small staircase that attached to the bed-frame.

Grigsby dressed in Gucci loafers and a kimono that Ryuki gifted him years ago. He phoned Ryuki on the intercom and told him to make three pots of coffee, warm up some donuts and make "healthy looking stuff that won't make me ill." Ryuki said Ira and his paralegals were still sleeping.

Downstairs Grigsby walked the long halls of Pemberton Manor and stopped in his tracks when he smelled something...organic. Scents of granola, body odor, and vanilla incense lingered.

"Ryuki! Why does it smell like the entire city of Burlington down here?" Grigsby shouted down the hall. He rounded the corner and saw a man lying on the couch in front of the fire place. The man had a long set of black and blonde dreadlocks and wore a sleeveless shirt. "Who the hell are you?" Grigsby asked.

The man looked at Grigsby, his eyes were thin and red and his mouth set agape.

"Hey dude," The man replied slowly. "I'm friends with BB-Cakes,"

"Who?"

"Oh right," the man giggled, "Becky, we met at Coachella,"

Ryuki walked into the room holding a silver tray containing a stack of donuts, wheatgrass shots and a pot of coffee. Grigsby abandoned the conversation with the stoned man on the couch and ran over to Ryuki. He took a shot of wheatgrass and grabbed a donut.

"Where is she?" Grigsby asked.

"The barn sir, she's riding one of the horses," Ryuki answered.

"Okay," Grigsby bit into the donut, "Take that thing and have him showered in the guest of guest's bathroom. Dress him in something that isn't made of hemp."

"Very well sir and where should I tell Ira you ran off to?"

"To the barn to see my daughter!" Grigsby stormed out.

CHAPTER FIFTEEN
Meet Becky

Becky Pemberton ran a stiff brush along her horse named Waldo. The flower crown she brought back from Coachella fell off in the middle of her ride which made her upset. She tried posing for a selfie in front of Waldo without the crown. His calico coat complements her strawberry blonde hair. Waldo kept moving, and Becky soon gave up.

The barn is where Becky launched her social media influencer career. She had Ryuki construct a floral backdrop in the barn. Then, clad in high waist jean shorts, bikini top, and a felt prospector's hat, she posed for her first photo. #FlowerGal #Blessed. Overnight Becky rose to social media fame. Skinny Detox Tea companies signed her for six-figure sponsorship deals. She modeled for obscure yoga start-ups and sneaker brands from Los Angeles. Becky was riding high until the market became saturated. Soon there were similar Beckys everywhere, and the deals dried up.

Since the fall from fame (and follower count), she's

been trying to claw back to that level. It looked like she was about to succeed five months ago. She had Ryuki run a focus group with Madison Avenue advertising firms and found an emerging niche— obscure stomach ailments. Becky began posting recipes for vegan gluten-free, dairy-free, soy-free, locally made kombuchas. Grigsby, her father, drank them by the gallon when she told him it was a healthy cocktail.

Things were going well again for Becky. Until the ides of March. That day all the other influencers banded together to expose Becky Paige Pemberton. They found proof that Becky was in fact not gluten intolerant or even lactose intolerant. Since then she's been persona non-grata by the people who preach positivity and well-being.

Feeling dejected once again, Becky took the family jet to Coachella to reconnect with herself. She spent $11,000 of her trust money on outfits. Another $20,000 went to supplies. This included a safari tent, a Tempurpedic mattress, marble vanity and other plush amenities. Here she found her truth...and Phoenix, a strapping 6'5" DJ who had hazel eyes, stonelike cheekbones, and dreadlocks. He'd never lifted a weight in his life but looked like he spent all day in the gym. She climbed on his shoulders during a set from a new tropic-techno-house band, and they fell in love.

Becky wondered if Phoenix was up from his post-yerba matte tea nap. She looked outside the barn and saw Grigsby marching toward her, his face red as a beet. Becky tossed a saddle on Waldo and readied her escape.

CHAPTER SIXTEEN

The Doughnut Thief

Grigsby was holding a doughnut when he entered the barn. "Becky, where are you?" He called out looking inside the stalls. There were only some horses staring blankly at him and his doughnut. Then he heard something from the back of the barn. Grigsby held the doughnut in his mouth and sprinted for the exit.

Becky leaped onto the saddle, but Grigsby grabbed hold of the reigns. "Shoot," Becky said, sounding defeated.

Waldo, the horse, looked at Grigsby, they were inches from each other's face. In an instant, Waldo snatched the doughnut from Grigsby's mouth, chomping it apart. Grigsby stared at Waldo's teeth that looked like a hallway of yellowish brown motel doors devouring the doughnut.

"Dammit, Waldo! That was mine."

Becky tried not to laugh but failed. Grigsby glared at up her.

"Ryuki just made them. I'm sending Waldo to the glue factory."

"Capital punishment for the doughnut thief? That doesn't sound fair."

"Forget it. Who's the guy with the muppet growing out of his head? Why is he on my couch?"

Becky sighed, "That's Phoenix Wright, we met at Coachella, he—"

"Wait, Wright? As in Wright Confectionary Company?" Grigsby asked.

"Um, yeah. The cake company, why?"

Grigsby grabbed the saddle horn and heaved himself on Waldo. Becky held on to his belt while he galloped the horse back to the manor.

CHAPTER SEVENTEEN

The Stallion in the Corridor

The floors of Pemberton Manor mimic the patterns of Istanbul's Hagia Sophia and various elements from St. Peter's Basilica. The marble tile is from Carrara, Italy. The stone was reclaimed from an abandoned monastery in Northern Scotland. They're beautiful but best of all, indestructible. Grigsby knew this when he rode into the halls on Waldo with his daughter, Becky, hanging on.

"Phoenix! Show yourself." Grigsby announced to the empty halls. They passed family oil paintings and a Cézanne. The stallion's shoes echoed like distant snare drums. Patina mirrors in gold frames gave the hall a heavenly look.

A confused and recently bathed man walked into view from the guest of guest's bathroom wing. He wore strange yoga pants where the crotch begins at the knee which give it a kangaroo look. For a moment though Phoenix looked like Michelangelo's David, except with worse hair.

Grigsby rode up to Phoenix. Becky leaped off the horse and ran to Phoenix's side.

"Phoenix Wright," Grigsby said.

"Um, yes, sir. That's me."

"Of Wright Confectionary Company?"

"Yep, my dad runs it. You like them Mr. P?"

Grigsby scoffed, "I don't eat anything wrapped in cellophane, I'm not an animal."

Phoenix frowned.

"Dad don't be a jerk,"

"Phoenix, does your family's company produce meat pies?"

"Meat pies?"

"Yes, meat pies, well they're called piroshki, Putin loves them apparently. I recently acquired a piroshki company and needed a distribution network."

Ryuki walked into the hall, still holding the silver tray. He informed Grigsby that Ira and the paralegals were having brunch and waiting for him. Grigsby said he'd be there soon. He hopped off of Waldo and handed Ryuki the reigns. "Bring Waldo back to the barn."

Becky looked at Grigsby, "Dad, I know a pie influencer on Insta—"

"Stop it right there; I don't want to hear about them. Influencers are your generation's Mary Kay, before that it was the Tupperware scammers, they're all the same." Grigsby said. "Phoenix I need you to do two things, or I'll have Crockett take you out of here."

"Who's Crockett?" Phoenix asked. Becky elbowed him and shook her head.

"You need to put on a shirt, preferably one with buttons and sleeves, if you're going to dine with us. Then I need you to get your father on the phone," Grigsby paused and thought for a moment. "And I'll have Ryuki bring you a stovepipe hat to cover the plant life growing out of your scalp." Phoenix tapped his dreads looking even more confused now.

Grigsby phoned Ryuki and requested enough coffee to wake up a small cartel village. The legal team will have to be fully alert for Grigsby's new plan.

CHAPTER EIGHTEEN

Caitlyn from Yale

Caitlyn, Ira's paralegal, sat and drank coffee while contemplating the decisions that brought her here. She was on her third cup in the Pemberton dining room trying to recap the night before.

In the last 18 hours she and her inept colleague, Peter, had been driven to the Manor. She saw a quiet Japanese butler incapacitate two Russian men with the stealth of an assassin. Then she watched a giant in samurai armor take out an angry Russian known only as The Bear. And then she saw them float away in a hot air balloon from the guest room window during sunrise.

Caitlyn knew that being top of her class at Yale Law would lead her to the thrones of power, but she did not expect it to be so... Roman. She thought the use of physical force, opulence, and never-ending feasts were a thing of the past. Caitlyn looked up at Grigsby. He sipped coffee as he negotiated with an attractive stoner named Phoenix. Caitlyn had to turn her seat askew to avoid staring at Phoenix's shoulders. Phoenix's father was on the

48

line, and they were talking about meat pies or something. Caitlyn found it hard to follow; she was distracted by everything. The artisan coffee, the opulence of the room, Phoenix's hazel eyes.

Caitlyn looked over at Becky who she followed on Instagram during her rise to fame. Becky seemed nice, in a ditsy-no-limit-trust-fund kind of way. She met plenty of girls like her when she did Harvard undergrad. Rich kids who go full tilt granola, they're called *Trustafarians*. Most of them dropped out to be avocado toast influencers. Caitlyn shrugged and figured it's better than the other ones she knew who were constantly offended.

"Great we can send Caitlyn. Ryuki packed her bags already. We can have her on the jet in two hours," Grigsby said.

Caitlyn, now fully alert, looked around the room. She had spaced out of the last half of the call. She hoped Ryuki hadn't found her Adderall and Dandelion chocolate bars.

"Um, point of inquiry..." she tried speaking in the corporate bullshit vernacular she'd been taught. Everyone stared at her. She grew quiet.

Grigsby continued, "Anyway, Ira will sort through the documents and Peter will join Caitlyn."

"Where am I going?" Caitlyn asked.

"Preston Wright, Phoenix's father, said he knows a guy who can supply our meat for the meat pies. He owns two slaughterhouses. You're going to meet him." Ira explained.

Grigsby chuckled, "Meet your meat."

"Okay, but where?" Caitlyn asked again, trying not to sound nervous.

Ira glared at her, "Johannesburg, South Africa."

CHAPTER NINETEEN

Golfing from Police

Grigsby hung up the phone and asked Becky and Phoenix to leave the room. Ira's paralegals, Caitlyn and Peter, were in the guest rooms preparing for their flight to South Africa. Grigsby and Ira were happy to have settled business matters before noon. They left the dining room and went to the roof to golf.

Ira teed off first, skimming the dogwood trees, banking between the pines and landing in Pemberton Pond. They were aiming for the various targets Ryuki had built on Grigsby's request. The targets are model ships; their sails have company logos that Pemberton Investments is at odds with. Ira's second shot knocked over the ship of the Bishop Company, an old prep school enemy.

Grigsby stepped up to the tee chomping on a cigar. "I see Phoenix in the gardens, $50 I can get it close enough to scare him."

"Don't do it Grigs, I don't want a lawsuit from the Wright family," Ira warned.

"Fair enough," Grigsby said, he teed off and struck a

model ship dead on.

Tears for Fears blared through the speakers but was interrupted by Ryuki's intercom message. "Sir, we've got someone at the gate who's demanding to see you,"

"Send them away. The only people I see without an appointment are John Daly, Angela Merkel or Warren Buffet." Grigsby continued a rant and Ryuki had to interrupt his master.

"Sir the police are here."

"How many police cars are at the gates?" Grigsby asked Ryuki through the intercom.

"Only one car sir, it looks like the sheriff's car," Ryuki answered.

"You're sure? What do the perimeter cameras read?"

"Sir, it's only one. If there was a raid on Pemberton Manor we'd know...and, we're prepared for such a day."

"This is why I love you Ryuki. I'll come meet them at the gates." Grigsby said.

Ira and Grigsby left the roof and headed for the motor pool. Ira grabbed a plate of doughnuts to bring the police, but Grigsby stopped him. "Get a new material Agent Cooper," Grigsby said. They climbed into the Gatsby Golf Cart. It's a bespoke golf cart made by the same designer who fashions all of Grigsby's cars. She's a former designer from Rolls Royce and quipped that this is her most decadent creation yet.

The golf cart looks like a 1920s Model T Ford. It's equipped with a cigar humidor, a golf shoe cleaner, and seat heaters. There's also a churro machine installed on it because "if you don't like Mexican cinnamon dough sticks you deserve a life of obscurity," Grigsby says.

Grigsby drove down the winding front drive of the

estate toward the gates. A tall man stood in front of a black SUV with a light bar on the roof. The gates opened and Grigsby drove the cart out.

"Mr. Pemberton," the man said.

"Yes, who are you? Where's Sheriff Maguire?" Grigsby asked.

"I'm Deputy Wilson?"

"Like the volleyball?"

"What?"

Grigsby smirked.

"Sir, I'm coming here as a courtesy on behalf of Sheriff Maguire. He's out of town right now."

"Go on Deputy,"

"It's about last night," Wilson paused. Grigsby held his tongue, a skill he learned at boarding school and from watching the O.J. Simpson trial: deny, deny, deny. "Sir...?"

As the Deputy began to explain, Grigsby and Ira couldn't hear what was being said. They both saw something behind the police officer. In the distance, climbing over the blue horizon. A hot air balloon. The Russians are back.

CHAPTER TWENTY

Missing Bunny

The hot air balloon climbed over the hill toward Grigsby, Ira and Deputy Wilson. Ira and Grigsby stood frozen in fear. The Russians won't be waving as they pass by in their wicker prison. Grigsby tried to remain calm and focus on the Deputy.

"There are witnesses saying that your car was at the Russian Tea Room last night in Manhattan?"

"That's correct," Grigsby said.

"Well, we they claim someone discharged a firearm at the car?" Deputy Wilson asked.

"Nonsense, check the car for yourself, nothing like that happened. The city is falling apart; it's regressing back to the 1970s, the mayor couldn't govern a Sleepys let alone a metropolis. Furthermore," Grigsby continued into a rant to buy time as he watched the hot air balloon approach.

Deputy Wilson noticed an oblong shadow growing behind him and turned to inspect. Ira and Grigsby held their breaths, waiting for The Bear to leap out and attack.

"Grigs, it's not them," Ira whispered. "Look,"

Deputy Wilson waved at the hot air balloon pilot, a sign attached to the lower basket read: CONNECTICUT HOT AIR BALLOON TOURS. The balloon sailed by them and continued on over the deep green pastures that bowed like a quiet tide. Ira let out a sigh of relief.

Grigsby thanked the Deputy for the heads up. Deputy Wilson said that he'd be sure to keep them apprised of any updates. He climbed into his SUV and drove off. Grigsby and Ira and returned to the manor where they found Ryuki waiting for them outside. He looked pale.

"Sir," Ryuki said with his head down, "We've received word from the Tahoe Residence..."

"And...?" Grigsby chuckled, "Did they run out of Chardonnay?"

"No sir, the staff informed me about your wife. She's missing."

CHAPTER TWENTY-ONE

The Cellar

"What do you mean missing?" Grigsby asked about his wife.

"Sir we received this new box of Cuban cigars in the mail this morning and found a note," Ryuki paused and looked at Ira and Grigsby, "I contacted the staff at the Tahoe Residence, and they confirmed she's gone."

"Gone?" Grigsby's knees felt weak and his mouth dry.

Ira grabbed Grigsby's underarm and held him upright, "Come on Grigs, let's get inside. We'll figure this out."

They entered the manor, and Grigsby sat on a long sofa with his head in his hands. Ryuki asked if he could get him anything. Grigsby shook his head solemnly.

He pictured his wife Bunny. Her green eyes and blonde hair, her laugh, the jean jacket she wore when they met in college, the smell of jasmine.

"We're going to get her back Grigs. Don't you worry." Ira said. "We have the resources we—"

Grigsby looked up, his eyes wide.

"What is it?" Ira asked.

Grigsby smirked for a moment, "We need to go the wine cellar, now."

"Oh Grigs, I don't think we should drink. Not now."

"We're not drinking, come on." Grigsby stood and called out to Ryuki saying there were heading for the cellar.

The duo descended into the lower levels of Pemberton Manor. They walked by Manet's Olympia and a Renoir upon approaching the wine cellar. Two silver knights stood in front of the oak doors. Grigsby scanned his eye, and the door opened an inch. He pushed it with all his weight. Inside the cellar, Grigsby walked through the long aisles until he found the Malbec section. Against a brick wall stood a shelf that holds the first Malbec's made in Mendoza.

"Grigs what's going on?" Ira asked as he watched his friend scan the shelves, pulling out some bottles.

Grigsby didn't speak, he pulled five bottles halfway off of their shelf and scanned for a bottle along the bottom row. Checking the labels, he made certain of the bottle before touching it. Then he yanked it out hard and the hiss of air compressing sounded, like a steam leak.

The shelf seemed to be moving backward. It halved and opened before them, and Grigsby walked through the new void. The temperature was colder a few feet beyond the shelf. An ancient door with a latch stood before them. Grigsby opened it, and they were then presented with a metal door that looked modern. He punched in a key code on a pad beside the door. It opened.

Ira followed Grigsby into a dark space that felt massive. Somewhere he heard water pattering. As amber lights lit up the area, Ira realized he was standing in an old elevator. It lowered and presented a sight he would never forget. Ira gasped.

Grigsby grinned, "Welcome to The Cavern, counselor."

CHAPTER TWENTY-TWO
Going Underground

Beneath Pemberton Manor is a place known as The Cavern. Only Grigsby and Ryuki have seen it. Today Ira, a longtime friend, and attorney, was entering it for the first time. His jaw agape he stared at the stalactites hanging from the bedrock ceiling.

"You built an actual bat cave," Ira said.

Grigsby was powering up the computer systems. "Not quite. First, there are no bats; I had them exterminated the minute I came down here. Who the hell would want blind rodents flying around carrying rabies? This is an inner sanctum. Second, I don't care about fighting crime like Batman did, I respect it, but it's not for me. Too much sweating involved. Plus, I like my face not getting bruised up."

"Fair enough," Ira looked at the mission control center that was powering up, "So what do you do down here?"

Grigsby climbed into a seat that looked like it belonged on the bridge of a spaceship. "I endure in my hobbies," Grigsby said, pointing to a screen that had a birds-eye view of a forest. "I monitor North Korea regularly and a few other investment properties. It's business and pleasure."

The jarring sound of the elevator startled Ira. Ryuki came walking into The Cavern holding a flight manifest.

"We don't need satellites, at least not yet. I'm looking for Bunny's fitness tracker. Ah, here we go." Grigsby logged onto a fitness website where there were images of people smiling while running and laughing while eating salads. "I got her this gadget last Christmas. It tracks your calories, steps, and all other ancillary crap, but it also has a GPS." Grigsby waited for the screen to load. "Bingo. We got her."

The computer screen showed a map of Lake Tahoe, and there was a green dot blinking at the North end of the lake. Grigsby thought about sending the coordinates to the staff at the Tahoe Residence but hesitated. "Ira, do you think we're compromised?"

Ira nodded, "I'd only trust the people in this cavern right now," Ira said.

Ryuki nodded in agreement.

"Okay men, let's do some digging and then we're flying out there," Grigsby held up the manifest, "The pilots are fine with the last minute notice?"

"Yes sir," Ryuki said.

"Good, good. Now let's find out who kidnapped my wife."

CHAPTER TWENTY-THREE
No Quarter

Ryuki retrofitted the Mercedes S600 with blue lights and sirens to make it look like the Governor is speeding by. Connecticut police don't want to pull over their boss's boss. This allows Grigsby to get to Manhattan in record time from Pemberton Manor. "Sheeple wait in traffic!" Grigsby usually shouts as they skirt by at high speeds making everyone dive out of the way.

He'd exercise this privilege to attend galas, shareholder meetings, Broadway shows, and bakery openings. Today was different. They were racing to a private airstrip where Grigsby's cocaine colored Learjet is waiting. Grigsby, Ira, and Ryuki are heading to Tahoe to find Grigsby's missing wife, Bunny Pemberton. Grigsby got a beat on her fitness tracker in the northern part of Lake Tahoe.

They pulled alongside the jet's red carpet. Grigsby loves red carpets in front of yachts, jets, and once in Thailand, elephants. A blonde flight attendant stood at the stairs with her hands together in front of a pencil skirt.

Her hair was pulled back tighter than piano wire. Grigsby saluted her and ran up the stairs. Ira's eyebrows bounced when he saw the flight attendant. Her scarlet lips and ocean eyes made it hard for him to breathe.

"Welcome aboard sir," She said holding out a manicured hand.

"Yes, hi, welcome aboard too," Ira said, "I mean, uh, thank you." He ran up the stairs after Grigsby, running away like a middle school boy at his first dance.

Ryuki did not even see the flight attendant. He ascended the staircase holding suitcases, focused on the next 24 hours. Ryuki's mission is clear: Find Bunny at all costs. Everything else around him is meaningless.

As they settled into their plush seats, the flight attendant delivered espressos and told them take off is in 20 minutes. "Make it 5 minutes, and I'll make sure this guy stops staring at you," Grigsby said. She smiled and went to the cockpit.

Grigsby pulled out a couple of items. Top 100 Executive lists from various business magazines and his boarding school yearbook. He looked at Ryuki and Ira. "We're making a list of suspects."

CHAPTER TWENTY-FOUR
Borderlands

At night the city of Reno looks like a small electric grid surrounded by darkness. Grigsby's Learjet landed at Reno-Tahoe International and scurried to a hanger. Ryuki loaded the bags into the special SUV that was waiting for them. Pemberton Investments has backed several successful tech companies. One of which is a skunkworks for the military. Grigsby phoned the founder and requested one of their SUVs. The interior looks more like the inside of NASA's Lunar Module than something driven by soccer moms.

Ira said goodbye to the flight attendant he'd fallen in love with. He never even got her name. She kissed him on the cheek which made him nearly faint.

Grigsby examined the list of suspects one more time before storing it in his briefcase. "Let's move," he said. Ryuki drove the SUV through the tiny city which was lit up like a flamboyant model train set.

"What a strange place," Ira said.

Grigsby nodded rubbing his five o'clock shadow. "It

looks like Peewee Herman's nightmares. I hate Reno."

Ira shrugged, "There's good sushi near Circus Circus,"

"Raw fish in a desert, sign me up."

They rode in silence for a long time on flat plains. Soon they climbed the precipitous hairpin roads toward Truckee. The SUV humped along in near vertical traffic. It lulled everyone, except Ryuki, asleep. Grigsby fell asleep with a peanut butter and jelly in his mouth.

After leveling out to the even ground, they approached Lake Tahoe. The ride felt smooth again. Ira jarred awake from vibrations in his side. He pulled a phone from his jacket pocket which was now ringing. "This isn't mine?"

Ryuki glanced at the rearview mirror and smacked his hand against the steering wheel. "I knew that flight attendant didn't seem right."

Grigsby woke up and spat out his PP&J onto his lap. He opened the window and tossed it. "What's the ruckus about?" Grigsby asked.

Ryuki looked at him through the mirror, "Sir, the kidnappers are calling."

CHAPTER TWENTY-FIVE

More Than Money

The voice came through the orphaned phone sounded like it was speaking from the bottom of a well. It was some sort of voice changing device.

"Hello Grigsby," the voice said.

"How much will it cost to get my wife back?" Grigsby said trying to remain calm.

The voice chuckled, "Money isn't all I want. I'm simply calling to say hello and tell you Bunny is fine. For now, that is."

"Here's the deal asshole, the less harmed she is, the more money you'll get, I—"

Bunny's scream interrupted Grigsby. He grew red with rage. "Bunny! I'm coming for you,"

The line went dead.

Ryuki, Ira, and Grigsby sat in silence for a moment. Ryuki tapped the navigation screen which zeroed in on a green dot which was Bunny's fitness tracker.

"Sir, the dot hasn't moved, we're less than an hour away," Ryuki said.

Grigsby exhaled, "Okay okay, good, where are we meeting your friends?"

"They're prepping at a motel nearby," Ryuki said.

"Good," Grigsby said sitting back. He looked out the window at the starry night and prayed that Bunny was okay. Ryuki called his close knit of friends to come help. They're all former military and have worked for Ryuki since they began at Pemberton Investments. This elite group of men and women typically secure new properties the company acquires in the developing world. No one knows about them. Grigsby calls them his ninjas.

They drove on wet roads with tall trees. A neon sign burned into the night down the road. It read MOTEL. As if that were something to boast about. In the parking lot were three Land Rover Defenders, all black, with metal grates across the windows.

"What are these guys hunting? Dinosaurs?" Grigsby asked.

"They're prepared for anything Sir," Ryuki said. They pulled into the parking lot. One of the doors opened, and a man in all black stepped out. He looked like a clone of Ryuki except his hair was a graying buzz cut.

"That's Akio," Ryuki said. They popped the car doors open and walked over to him.

He gave a curt nod. "Come inside. We don't have much time."

CHAPTER TWENTY-SIX

She's a Ghost

The motel room had the same smell found in every motel in America: musk, mildew and the lingering scent of urine. Grigsby did not sit; he wanted only the soles of his Gucci loafers to touch the room. Inside were three operators from Pemberton Investments. Akio is their team leader. The two others are Keisha and Luke.

"This is it?" Grigsby asked. "Doesn't look like the A-Team."

"Not quite, I have sent the rest of the team to setup a perimeter around where we believe Bunny Pemberton is," Akio explained. He motioned to a laptop that sat above a browning TV. "With the perimeter secured, we were able to pinpoint the fitness tracker location. It's currently inside an old cabin."

"Any vehicles spotted coming or going?" Grigsby asked.

"No. There are no means of transport at the cabin which leads us to believe this a drop off point. Nothing permanent." Akio answered. "The plan is to head up there soon. Keisha will be our ghost."

Ira and Grigsby looked at her. She gave a wolfish smile. "I can go anywhere without being seen."

"Once she confirms what's inside we'll know what we're dealing with," Akio said. "Questions? No? Good. Let's move."

The convoy of Land Rover Defenders drove through back country roads, leading the way. Ryuki, Grigsby, and Ira followed in their SUV. A mile from the target they shut their headlights off and continued in the pitch of the night. "I learned to drive blind from Akio," Ryuki said smiling. Grigsby and Ira held on to roof handles and didn't say anything.

Soon they were 100 yards from cabin according to the navigation system. Ira squinted into the night and tried to see. Grigsby reached under the seat and pulled out a set of night vision binoculars. Ira gave him an incredulous look.

"A man with means and curiosity should always travel with these," Grigsby said.

He was able to see the cabin; it's small structure hid well in the dense trees. Grigsby didn't see any of Akio's men but was assured they were out there. The pines and firs smelled stronger in the night air. Grigsby took long breaths to keep calm.

"Keisha's heading for the cabin," Akio announced over the radio. The car remained quiet.

Minutes which felt like hours crept by. Then a live video from Keisha's helmet camera streamed to the SUV's screens. They watched her climb with the grace of a gymnast through a cabin window. Keisha checked every room. All empty. Ryuki punched the steering wheel. Then the camera focused on an item. Keisha bent over to pick up. She held it to the camera and Grigsby saw it was Bunny's fitness tracker.

Keisha sighed, "She was here, but now she's gone now."

CHAPTER TWENTY-SEVEN

Breadcrumbs

Akio and his team invited Grigsby and Ira into the cabin where they found Bunny's fitness tracker. Keisha handed the fitness tracker to Grigsby. He cherished it for a minute, thinking of his wife, wondering if she's okay. The rest of the team inspected the cabin, looking for any clues.

Grigsby sat on in a wicker seat which had threadbare plaid cushions. He examined the fitness tracker. "C'mon Bunny, where are you?"

Akio stepped back into the room. "We couldn't find much; this place must have been an interim waypoint for them."

"What now?" Ira asked.

"The ball is unfortunately in their court. We're going to have to wait for their call again. I suggest we get back to Truckee; there's better cell reception there."

Grigsby remained silent.

"Grigs? You okay" Ira asked.

Grigsby smiled wide, like a kid on Christmas morning. "I knew you'd do it Bunny," He said to the tracker.

Grigsby held it up to Ira and Akio. Scratched into the band read the letter R. "We have our lead gentlemen. Let's get that list of suspects."

Ryuki came sprinting from the SUV with Grigsby's briefcase. They turned on the kitchen light in the cabin and pulled out the suspect list they made on the plane. It looked like the casting sheet for a Brooks Brothers catalog, a litany of waspy names. They scanned the last names starting with the letter R and found nothing. They looked at first names only.

"Sonofabitch," Ira said.

"Randolph," Grigsby growled. "Randolph Scout Bishop." Akio glanced at the name and began searching it on his laptop.

"How do you know him?" Akio asked.

"We played lacrosse together back in boarding school, the prick was a hoover, but I'd outscore him. Anyway, we've been business rivals for a long time." Grigsby said.

Akio typed for a while without saying anything. Grigsby tried coloring in the past and seeing where he'd crossed him to the point where he'd consider doing something this rash. Akio interrupted him, "Sir, we have his jet's recent flight manifest."

"And?"

"He's here in Tahoe."

CHAPTER TWENTY-EIGHT

The Randolph Raid

"How far are we?" Grigsby asked as the SUV sped through back roads outside Truckee.

"We're getting close, Akio's team has the home already surrounded, they've confirmed he's inside. No one else is in the ski house." Ryuki said.

Pines flashed by as they made the turn onto the long drive toward Randolph Scout Bishop's ski house. They were 300 yards from the gate when Akio radioed them.

"We see Randolph on the second floor, no guards in sight, should we move in?" Akio asked.

"Go, move fast, don't kill him," Grigsby answered.

The SUV slowed as they watched the team move in like a brigade of wraiths in the night. All that was visible were red laser beams and green tint of their goggles. Shouting ensued moments later. Smoke and sparks erupted from the front door as the team breached it.

Ira and Grigsby watched the raid through the monitors in the SUV. A few of the team members had their cameras on. The video feeds were shaky but showed the team moving fast through a well-appointed ski house. Classic ski posters were framed on the walls, and a roaring fire crackled. The team heard something upstairs and scaled the stairs faster than a hyperactive poodle.

Screaming could now be heard through the video feed. They kicked down the door to find Randolph Scout Bishop wearing a sailor's hat and nothing else with a blonde woman in bed. Grigsby was biting down so hard he felt his molar crack. The team instantly shot Randolph with tasers. He vibrated like a flag in a storm and fell off the bed, limp. They cuffed him and checked on the woman who was still wailing.

"Bunny!" Grigsby opened the door of the SUV and sprinted for the house. Ira and Ryuki followed. No one had ever seen Grigsby move that fast before. Minutes later he was scaling the same stairs he saw on the video feed. Screams and cries still bore out from the room. Grigsby feared the worst. He ran in to see a blonde woman holding a comforter over herself. The team was trying to calm her down while Randolph lay unconscious on a Zebra skin rug.

Grigsby walked in, stepped on the bed and without saying a word stared at the woman. She stopped screaming and looked up at a sweaty, out of breath, pastel-clad man. "Who the hell are you?" She asked.

Grigsby ignored her, "Team, meet Miss Alabama, Randolph's mistress."

CHAPTER TWENTY-NINE

Bulls in the China Shop

The next hour was complicated. Grigsby's team, who raided the Bishop ski house, were now surveying the scene. They were tasked with putting together an estimate of damages they caused. The costliest items seemed to be the 70-year-old oak door that lay in smithereens. Plastic explosives were used to breach it. And a flash-bang grenade broke a shelf of Mrs. Bishop's China Set from 1923. Grigsby agreed it was overkill.

"Lloyds of London is going to have a field day," Ira said.

Grigsby sat with his head in his palms. "Not to mention Randolph's legal team. You have any idea how we'll defend against this?"

"I'll take care of it. It's going to cost you, and it'll sting, but it can go away." Ira said, patting Grigsby on the back.

"Grigsby, you son of a bitch!" Randolph shouted from the other room. Members of his team were treating him after they tasered him into submission. Grigsby felt perturbed. Not because he destroyed the house of a perennial rival, but he was still no closer to finding Bunny.

"Guess he's regained consciousness now." Ira quipped. "You don't have to talk to him."

"I don't want to."

"Good. What are we going to do about the mistress?"

"What all mistresses want when they're exposed?" Grigsby asked.

"Another sugar daddy?"

"Money. Go talk to her."

Ira went to the room where Miss Alabama sat wiping off her makeup. She was now clothed in a cable-knit sweater and jeans. Her hair was so bleached it looked like the steamed napkins that are doled out at Sushi restaurants. She looked into the mirror and saw Ira and smiled. Twenty minutes later Ira came out with a signed NDA and a note of "needs" Miss Alabama has. He handed it to Grigsby.

"Jesus, she must think I'm Santa. What the hell is a Pomsky?"

"It's a cross-breed of a Pomeranian and a Husky; they're actually quite cute—"

"Pay it."

Ryuki came running into the room with his phone out, "Sir it's the kidnappers."

CHAPTER THIRTY
Grigsby & Karl The Fog

The call was brief. The kidnappers told Grigsby to be in San Francisco by noon. He'd provide the location and then said, "Bring your lawyer too, we'll need him." This is something Grigsby couldn't connect. What would they want with Ira?

The convoy loaded up and headed west for San Francisco through the switchback roads. The double yellow line stretched to the horizon beside dense pines. Grigsby told Akio and his team to keep their distance when they arrive in the city. They haven't been as helpful as he hoped. Grigsby compared it to hiring hyenas to build a wedding cake. Then he leaned back and told Ira to wake him when he sees Karl the Fog; a name San Franciscan's gave the fog.

Entering the city of San Francisco from the northern Marin Headlands is special. It feels like you're falling, fast, out of a Renoir painting as the highway spits you out toward the Golden Gate Bridge. Brilliant shades of emerald, coral, and blue blend together through the gray and white fog.

Grigsby gave Karl the middle finger. One summer Grigsby ran his yacht aground after being wrapped in dense fog. Now that the fog has a name, he hated him.

The convoy drove across the Golden Gate Bridge. They could only see red art deco pillars of the bridge; the rest was in the fog. It felt like driving into a sinister land. A place that's not quite an oblivion but on the edge.

The phone buzzed with a text message from a blocked number. It read, "Clift Hotel, Room 39. Grigsby and Ira only." Ryuki radioed the team, telling them to set a wide perimeter and to stay out of sight. Grigsby's SUV drove into the city. Ira stared out the window and saw the tent cities adjacent billion dollar tech companies. A naked crackhead danced across Market Street; bystanders ignored him like it was a pigeon.

"Such a strange city," Ira commented.

Grigsby sighed, "In a city that will not tolerate inefficiencies like slow internet and on-demand limos, sushi, and TV; it's incredible to see the same populace tolerate crime, homelessness, and filth."

Ira nodded and wondered why the same companies that preach purpose over profit had fecal matter lining their office borders.

The SUV stopped, and a man in black opened the door. "Welcome to the Clift Hotel gentlemen."

CHAPTER THIRTY-ONE

Room 39

Grigsby and Ira walked fast through the lobby, ignoring the welcome of the front desk clerk. The security guard by the elevators waved them through without saying a word. "A bespoke tailored suit is the ultimate passport," Grigsby said as the elevator doors closed.

Ira nodded, he seemed more nervous than usual.

"You clear on the plan?" Grigsby asked.

"I feel like we're walking into the lion's den."

"We are."

The doors opened, and they followed the patterned carpets through a darkened hallway. Faith Evans could be heard humming through the walls of another guest's room. They're having a more pleasant evening Grigsby thought. They stopped at Room 39 and knocked twice.

A short Mexican man answered the door. His body was checkered in patterned tattoos; he looked like one big Vans sneaker. The man ushered Grigsby and Ira into the bathroom and frisked them. "Okay," he said after, holding out his hand, "Go in."

The duo continued down the long corridor of the suite. Grigsby noticed a series of orange extension cords running along the floor toward the living room. It connected to a variety of computer monitors setup atop a dresser. One screen was blank; the other was a video feed a woman inside of what looked to be a shipping container. It was Bunny. She was pacing the room like a caged dog.

They entered the room. Three men stood there, all with severe sunburns and cracked lips. The condition of the men delayed Grigsby recognizing who they were. The center man removed a pair of cataract sunglasses to expose red and gray-blue eyes.

"Hello, Grigsby."

Grigsby said nothing. He remembered the fitness band Bunny left in the cabin. The letter R wasn't complete; she was trying to spell the letter B. It all came together as Grigsby stood before The Bear. This time though, he held all the cards.

CHAPTER THIRTY-TWO

The Contract

Grigsby stood before The Bear. On the screen beside them showed a live view of Bunny Pemberton who was locked away inside a shipping container. She was lying down now. Grigsby stared at the sunburnt Russians and smirked.

"How long were you up in the balloon for?" Grigsby asked.

"A day and a half you prick—" said one of the men. The Bear held up a hand, and he stopped.

"Listen Pemberton. I call the shots; I'm in charge. Anything happens to me again; I'll act on my insurance policy." The Bear said, motioning to the screen.

"You've gone too far this time. You're lucky my team isn't here skinning you." Grigsby seethed.

"Instead of this back and forth, why don't we get this over with?" Ira said.

Grigsby nodded. The Bear shrugged.

One of The Bear's men pulled out a manila envelope and tossed it on the table. Grigsby and Ira examined the documents.

"The pie company? The vodka company?" Grigsby asked.

The Bear nodded.

"This can't be all you want. What else is there? There's always something else."

The Bear smiled, "I want both of those companies and a board seat on Pemberton Investments."

"You prick, do you think I'd allow you inside my empire?"

Ira nudged Grigsby and pointed at the screen. The door to the shipping container opened. A group of men were entering, the screen went blank for a moment, and then Bunny was gone.

"Where'd she go? Where'd she go?!" Grigsby tried leaping over the table, but Ira held him back.

"You can see your wife tonight or, well, there's the other way." The Bear said.

"Grigs, listen to him." Ira urged.

Grigsby said nothing for a long time. Then he picked up the documents and looked at The Bear. "I want assurance that she's okay. Have your men arrange a meeting place, once my team sees she's unharmed. I'll sign."

The Bear smiled and nodded to one his men. The man called and spoke in Russian. "Tell your team to head to Fort Mason. In a half hour, don't be late."

CHAPTER THIRTY-THREE
The Exchange

Inside Room 39 no one spoke. Grigsby stared at The Bear. They were waiting for the teams to rendezvous at Fort Mason. Ira read the contracts over again. When Bunny Pemberton is safe, Grigsby will sign them. This will give The Bear full ownership of the pie company, vodka company and place him on the board of Pemberton Investments.

Grigsby's phone rang, it was Akio, he answered and turned on the speakerphone. "We're at Fort Mason. What are the next steps?"

The Bear grinned. "Leave your weapons in the cars and walk into warehouse B."

Akio said nothing.

The Bear repeated himself.

"Grigsby?" Akio said.

"Do it," Grigsby grunted.

"Copy, stay on the line," Akio said. He ordered his men to disarm and head to the warehouse. Minutes later Akio spoke, "We're inside, Bunny Pemberton is in sight."

Grigsby sat at the end of his seat. The Bear motioned to the fountain pen on the table. Grigsby grabbed the pen and held it above the documents.

"Let her go," The Bear said on his phone.

Time slowed. No one spoke. All you could hear were soft footsteps. Then Akio spoke, "We got her."

Grigsby immediately signed both documents and pushed them across the table. "Get her out fast," Grigsby ordered. You could hear the team running now, a rhythm of heavy boots striking the damp pavement. Then the popping of car doors.

"We're in the convoy, heading out, see you at the rendezvous," Akio said. Grigsby hung up.

Grigsby stood and buttoned his jacket. "We're done here. I'm going to see my wife."

"Hang on a second," Ira said, "What about my payment?"

The Bear and Grigsby gave Ira a confused look.

"My firm completed all the legal work for both companies you're now the sole owner of. Since today was conducted in an unusual sense of expediency, I demand my cut."

Grigsby grabbed Ira's shoulder and leaned into his ear, "Are you seriously doing this right now?"

"I want my money," Ira said, staring at The Bear.

The Bear laughed, "You're greedier than I am."

Ira slammed his fist on the table, "Fuck you pay me." Ira said. "Take it from the Pemberton Investment salary you're now getting."

"You're some friend," Grigsby said.

The Bear opened his laptop and spoke to one his men in Russian and sighed, "Fine, fine. Give me your bank account number."

CHAPTER THIRTY-FOUR
Mariachi Bands & Pig Roasts

Ryuki drove the SUV out of the city aimed toward Napa. Akio's team brought Bunny to her favorite vineyard for the recovery process. "Wine heals all wounds." She said during their first vineyard tour years ago. Akio agreed that a rural environment would be safer too.

"That's correct, yes both companies, run the trace and you'll see what I'm talking about. Okay, thanks." Ira hung up his phone and looked at Grigsby. "FBI and Homeland are at the Clift Hotel; they intercepted 3 Russian terrorists."

Grigsby gave a wild grin, "Excellent. Will the charges stick?"

Ira nodded, "Funding terrorist organizations is sent right up the chain."

"How'd you get a hold of a terrorist group's bank account numbers anyway?" Grigsby asked.

"I know people who've defended questionable clients."

"Three birds with one stone, well-done sir, this removes The Bear from the Board. You were great back there."

Ira chuckled, "I didn't come off too greedy?"

Grigsby smiled and looked out the window. The rolling pastures carried fastidiously arranged vines over green hills. Cows watched them drive by with little interest. They must see as many cars as the drivers see cows.

Ryuki drove slowly down the dirt road toward the vineyard. The only vehicles in the lot were Akio's team. Grigsby climbed out and entered the elegant winemaker's hall. The room was lined with purple stained casks and gleaming wine glasses. Akio and spoke to a woman in a blue and white sundress; she turned to face the arriving guests. Grigsby, at a loss of words, embraced Bunny for several minutes. No one in the room spoke. Bunny let her tears dry on Grigsby jacket.

The popping of a champagne cork halted the moment. Ira approached with two flutes in hand. Both Bunny and Grigsby downed them in one shot and returned them back to Ira. Bunny demanded a pig roast. When the vineyard owner explained, that wasn't possible she told Akio's team to go hunting. They obliged.

That evening a pig spun over bonfire flames. Grigsby hired a mariachi band to play until sunrise. Ira danced. Ryuki did too; his face was redder than a taillight from slamming back Merlots. Becky and Phoenix arrived too; her parents omitted what had happened.

Akio and the team patrolled the grounds and kept watch over the Pembertons. They realized it was gratuitous. Bunny's hand hadn't left Grigsby since they reunited. Grigsby stared into Bunny's green eyes and promised always to keep her safe. She handed him an empty plate and motioned to the chef carving up the pig. Grigsby smiled, and they ate like royalty that night. Life's simplest pleasures are accentuated during feasts. Grigsby agreed it's all meaningless without friends and family.

July 4, 2017 - August 7, 2017
San Francisco, California
Palm Springs, California

Grigsby will be back soon.

Afterward

Grigsby Ives Pemberton is a force of nature and doesn't deserve to be constrained to a singular storyline. That's why I'm writing several more Grigsby stories. Every day they'll debut on my website robertmaisano.com.

You can receive updates on this series and my forthcoming books by joining my community. Sign up on that page, and I'll send you a free book on why we all need fiction. Also, if you have story ideas let me know, happy to give you credit.

Thank you for reading. In a world of endless content, deciding to read my writings is the ultimate compliment which I do not take lightly. I will always strive to provide great stories.

About The Author

Robert Maisano is a writer, speaker, and award-winning marketer. He's written for Business Insider and Thought Catalog. Every day he publishes a new Grigsby story on robertmaisano.com. He lives in San Francisco.

A Note On The Type

The typeface used throughout the novella is a serif design from the 1750s created by John Baskerville in Birmingham, England which was then cut into metal by John Handy (appropriate name).

The style is classified as a transitional typeface. Earlier designs of the typeface increased the contrast between thick and thin strokes, which make the serifs a bit more tapered and sharper. Baskerville is one of the many popular typefaces used in book design.

A non-scientific study conducted in 2012 asserted that readers of the Baskerville typeface increased the likelihood of the reader agreeing with the prose by 1.5% when compared to other fonts such as Georgia, Helvetic, Trebuchet, and the ever so silly Comic Sans.

Now if you ever meet a designer or a calligrapher you have a nice tidbit of information that'll make you appear wiser in front of them.

Biplane Media

BOOKS | FILM | RADIO
SF • NYC

At Biplane Media, we support creatives who make perennially stunning content. We're dedicated to capturing adventure in everyday life and finding the wonder that hides around the world.

The gatekeepers are gone. As access to digital mediums proliferates throughout the world, it's easier for us to distribute our art to you. We don't have to rely on getting picked by a top publishing house or major studio. We can show our art as easily as we can make it now.

What does this all mean?

Since we're independent and at the forefront of content distribution, we promise to price our work accordingly. The goal is to make it as accessible as possible. The entire *Grigsby Series* is available online for free. If you enjoy what we make the highest compliment is to share it with friends. Spreading the word and growing this community will allow us to venture into more exciting projects.

If you're a creator and have something you'd like to share, we'd be happy to chat. Drop by our site: www.biplane.media to get in touch. Everyone has a story in them, we're here to help tell it.

Bonus Content

The next few pages have a free preview of the next novella in the *Grigsby Series*.

Picaroon Coast, is the second novella in the series and will debut in the Fall of 2017.

Grigsby is circumnavigating the globe aboard his yacht, the *Narwhal*. As his ship is bearing through the Arabian Sea toward the Gulf of Aden, a group of Somalian pirates attack. A series of events unfold that send Grigsby, Ira, and Ryuki ashore.

They're picked up by a group of bandits who bring them to a horrifying tribal village of headhunters. Now trapped, Grigsby must plan an escape before it's too late.

Read the first two chapters on the following pages.

CHAPTER ONE

Golfing at Sharks

Grigsby teed off of the deck of his 82-foot yacht named *Narwhal*. The golf ball sailed over ocean mist and bounced off the skin of a shark.

"Good shot sir," Ryuki called out from the helm. He spotted the sharks feeding and found it to be a prime opportunity to brush up on his long game.

"I'm the only shark in this ocean!" Grigsby called out as he set another ball down. After several more shots, he handed the club to Ryuki, insisting he give it a samurai swing. Grigsby took the helm. He looked out at the Africa coastline, it was low and the color of camel hide. The *Narwhal's* course is set for the Suez Canal, their destination is the island of Crete in Greece. Grigsby couldn't wait to have moussaka and that custard dessert he could never pronounce. Those thoughts faded when he saw something on the horizon.

Grigsby saw the pirates first. He used military binoculars to track a skiff that launched off the Somalian shores. Cursing, he tightened the mainsail and ordered Ryuki to raise the topsail and jib. They were going to need all the speed they can muster. The elegant yacht pitched and yawed over pale blue surf and still, the pirates were gaining.

Ira poked his head through a hatch with a sleeping mask against his forehead, "What's all the yelling about?"

"Get dressed man, pirates are heading for us," Grigsby answered.

Ira's eyes widened and he retreated to his quarters. Moments later he was topside, "What should we do?"

Grigsby ignored Ira and called for Ryuki who was radioing for help. "Get up here, we need to fend them off ourselves, I'm not ending up like Captain Phillips," Grigsby said.

Ryuki ran to the stern of the ship trying to gauge the distance between the approaching pirates. "Ira, go down below and bring up all the flares we have." Ryuki ordered. Ira nodded and disappeared below deck.

Grigsby piloted the *Narwhal* over high surf, maintaining a steady course. "Ryuki, can we use the New Year's cannon?"

They both looked at a brass cannon Grigsby had installed for a New Year's Eve party. Ryuki ran across the deck to inspect the cannon. He unlatched it and wheeled it to the stern.

"What can we use as ammo?" Ryuki asked.

"Kettlebells." Grigsby answered. His New Year's resolution was to attempt exercising twice a month.

"Ira bring up the kettlebells too." Ryuki called out.

The first gunshot rang out from the pirates. It punctured the sails making small holes. Ryuki pulled Grigsby down to take over. "It's a warning shot, but they could miss." They turned and saw the skiff was only 100 yards away. It was loaded with sinewy men in rags, holding rusty AK-47s.

Ira returned, holding a bag of flares and two kettlebells. He looked terrified.

Grigsby looked aft, "Men. Prepare to repel boarders."

CHAPTER TWO

Pirates

The pirates were closing in on the *Narwhal*, Grigsby's yacht. Grigsby maintained a beam reach across the Arabian Sea. The gleaming white mainsail bore a few new holes from the pirate's rifle fire. Grigsby chomped on his cigar as he ducked for cover.

"What's the status of the cannon?" Grigsby asked Ryuki who was loading the brass cannon with a kettlebell.

"Ready sir,"

"Good," Grigsby looked aft and noticed the skiff of Somalians were only 50 yards away, he could see their yellow eyes and machetes. "Commence firing on my mark." Grigsby brought in the sails and pointed upwind, gaining more speed and searching for calm waters. He looked aft once more and then shouted, "Fire."

The boom of the cannon reverberated off their chests. Everyone's ears were ringing. The kettlebell sailed through the air and missed the skiff by a few feet. Grigsby cursed and told Ryuki to reload.

"Ira give me one of the flare guns," Grigsby ordered. Ira obliged. Grigsby tucked the flare gun in the waistband of his Nantucket-red pants. "When they come closer, aim for the center of their skiff. "Ryuki how we doing?" The *Narwhal* climbed the azure surf and glided down each wave, spume and sea flooded from the bow and ran off the deck.

"Almost ready sir,"

"Fire at will. Don't miss this is one, it's our last shot."

"Yes sir,"

They could hear the pirates now, screaming above their engine. They were telling Grigsby to heave to. Grigsby shouted back, saying that no one, not even the IRS, will ever take his yacht. One pirate leaned off the skiff and shot at Grigsby, the bullet hit Ira and he fell to the deck.

That's when Grigsby's rage overtook him. "You bastards!" He pulled the flare gun out and steadied his aim at the skiff which bounced off the waves. Grigsby fired the flare and it connected with the stern, lighting it ablaze. Several pirates fell overboard. Grigsby didn't stop. He pushed Ryuki out of the way and leveled the cannon, waiting for the surf to settle. Then he fired. What happened next was devastating.

Continue Reading

All of the *Grigsby Series* stories can be found at www.robertmaisano.com.

Keep In Touch

Search my name into your favorite social network and say hi.

Robert Maisano